Library of Congress Cataloging in Publication Data
Delton, Judy.   Groundhog's day at the doctor.
SUMMARY: Groundhog visits the doctor and
dispenses his own medical advice while there.
[1. Animals—Fiction.   2. Medical care—
Fiction] I. Maestro, Giulio   II. Title
PZ7.D388Gr   [E]   80–36718
ISBN 0–8193–1041–7   ISBN 0–8193–1042–5 lib. bdg.

Groundhog's Day at the Doctor

by Judy Delton

pictures by Giulio Maestro

Parents Magazine Press
New York

For Jamie, my favorite son

Groundhog woke up and stretched.
"It must be February second,"
  he said. "Groundhog Day.
  I can't stay in bed any longer."

Groundhog climbed out of bed
and got dressed.
"My, I'm stiff," he said, yawning.
"I don't think I've had enough sleep."

After Groundhog drank some tea,
he sat in his chair and dozed off.

When he woke up, he still felt stiff.
And when he looked in the mirror,
he said, "Dear me. I am pale.
Perhaps I have the flu.
I'd better go and see the doctor."

So Groundhog put on his wool coat,
his hat, his muffler,
and his warm boots.
He started down the path.
Soon he arrived at the doctor's office.

Rabbit was sitting in a chair
waiting for the doctor.

"Why, good morning, Groundhog,"
whispered Rabbit.
"Hello, Rabbit," answered Groundhog.

"What is the matter with your voice,
   Rabbit?" asked Groundhog.
"I have a very sore throat.
   I can hardly talk," answered Rabbit.
"It all started with a head cold."

"Rabbit, Rabbit," said Groundhog.
"Were you out in the snow without
your boots?"

Rabbit thought a minute. Then he nodded.
"I believe I was, come to think of it.
Sunday night when I came from
Weasel's house, it was snowing."

"No wonder you are sick," said Groundhog.
"Have you tried a hot mustard footbath?"
  Rabbit shook his head.
"Why don't you try that?"
  said Groundhog kindly.
"It brought back Squirrel's voice."

"Why, thank you, Groundhog.
  I will," said Rabbit.
"The doctor isn't in yet,
  and it may be a long wait.
  I think I'll just do as you say."

A few minutes after Rabbit left,
Goose hobbled in, leaning on a cane.
"Dear me, Goose," said Groundhog.
"What ever happened to you?"

"I've just sprained my ankle," she said.
"It looks bad," said Groundhog,
  shaking his head.
"It is very swollen."

"My cousin had a sprained ankle.
Worse than yours, Goose, much worse.
He put cold mud packs on it,
and it was much better by evening.
The next morning he could walk.
But the mud is frozen now.
Why don't you try snow?"

"It may be a long wait for the doctor,
and my ankle is aching.
I think I'll just do as you say.
Thank you, Groundhog."

As Goose was leaving,
Chipmunk came in the door.
He had red spots all over
his face, paws, and tail.

He sat down on the stool
that Goose had just left.
Groundhog cleared his throat.
"What are those . . . er . . .
spots, Chipmunk?" he said.

"It's not the spots I care about,"
chattered Chipmunk.
"It's my stomach.
Oh, how it hurts!"

Groundhog held up a paw.
"Just a minute, Chipmunk.
Do you have a fever?"

Chipmunk felt his forehead.
"No," he said.
"Headache?" said Groundhog.
Chipmunk shook his head.
"Where were you last night?"
Groundhog asked finally.
"Last night," said Chipmunk,
"I went berry picking in the woods."

"Aha! Those spots are berry juice,"
said Groundhog.
"And did you eat too many berries,
Chipmunk?"
"Well, yes, I guess so," said Chipmunk.

"That happened to my grandfather once,"
said Groundhog, nodding his head.
"And do you know what he took?"
"What?" said Chipmunk anxiously.
"Baking soda in water," said Groundhog.
"He was better in no time, Chipmunk."

"Really?" said Chipmunk.
"Thank you, Groundhog.
I think I'll just do as you say.
It may be a long wait for
the doctor, and I do want to
get rid of this stomach ache."
So Chipmunk waved good-bye
and left.

Groundhog sat down again.
He picked up a magazine
and began to read.
Just then the doctor came in.

He looked around the room.
"Groundhog, you seem to be
my only patient this morning!
What can I do for you?"

"Dear me," said Groundhog.
"I forget what the matter was. . . .
  Oh, yes, I remember.
  I felt tired and stiff,
  and I looked pale."

"I'm surprised you're even out of bed,"
said the doctor.
"I always get up on Groundhog Day,"
answered Groundhog.

The doctor looked
at his calendar.
"Groundhog Day is tomorrow,"
he said.
"You are up early.
You know, my mother
used to feel stiff and tired
when she needed
fresh air and exercise.
That's what you need,
too, Groundhog."

"That makes sense," said Groundhog.
The doctor looked around and said,
"Since there are no more patients,
why don't we go skiing together?
I could use some exercise too."

"And afterwards we will go to my house,"
said Groundhog.
"I will fill two hot-water bottles.
MY mother always used to say that
heat was good for sore muscles."

ABOUT THE AUTHOR AND ARTIST

Although JUDY DELTON and GIULIO MAESTRO have never met, they share much in common. For one, they have the same birthday! Perhaps this gives them a similar way of looking at the world, for Mr. Maestro is an expert at interpreting Ms. Delton's stories.

Groundhog's Day at the Doctor is Mr. Maestro's first book for Parents, but he has illustrated four other Judy Delton titles for other publishers. He has illustrated many other children's books— some written by his wife, Betsy—and has written and illustrated others on his own.

Judy Delton is a busy writer and teacher. She has written over a dozen children's books, including *Rabbit's New Rug* for Parents, as well as many articles and essays. She now also teaches writing.

Ms. Delton lives in St. Paul, Minnesota. Mr. Maestro lives in Madison, Connecticut.